CONTENTS

Stories retold by Maureen Spurgeon

First published 1995 by Brown Watson
The Old Mill, 76 Fleckney Road,
Kibworth Beauchamp
Leicestershire, England

Reprinted 1996, 1997.

ISBN 0-7097-1026-7

Printed in the E.C.

FAIRY TALE TREASURY

BOOK FOUR

Brown Watson
ENGLAND

The Ugly Duckling

Mother Duck had found the perfect place on the farm to build her nest. It was cool and dry, with plenty of grass, yet close enough to a stream when the time came to take her ducklings for a swim. The other ducks quacked and splashed about in the water, as she sat waiting for her eggs to hatch.

Then, at last, came the great day when the shells burst open, one after the other!
"Cheep-Cheep!" piped the tiny, yellow ducklings as they waddled around. "How wide the world is!"

Mother Duck fussed round them proudly. She was so busy trying to keep all her ducklings together, that, at first, she did not notice there was one egg, bigger than any of the others, still in the nest.

"That's a turkey's egg!" quacked an old duck when she saw it. "And turkeys never learn to swim, my dear, not like our little ones. Nasty birds, they are, too! Take my advice and leave it alone."

But Mother Duck said she would sit on the egg a little longer until it hatched. And, instead of a pretty, yellow duckling, out came a fat, ugly chick with horrible dark grey feathers!

"Was this a turkey chick?" wondered Mother Duck, leading the way down to the stream. How glad she was to see the ugly little bird swimming along behind the others.

"He's not a turkey," she thought, "just an Ugly Duckling."
The Ugly Duckling soon began to grow, and as he grew, the uglier he became. The other ducklings wouldn't even talk to him.

The hens in the farmyard pecked at him whenever he came near. Worst of all was the turkey cock who came at the Ugly Duckling making loud gobbling noises, until it was red in the face.

Even the little girl who fed the farmyard birds aimed kicks at him. Unhappy and frightened, he flew off, some smaller birds getting out of his way. "That's because I'm so ugly," he thought.

The Ugly Duckling flew on until he came to a marsh where some wild ducks lived.
"My," said one, "you're so ugly!"
The Ugly Duckling just fluffed up his feathers and fell asleep.

Next day, the air was shattered by hunters shooting at the wild ducks. The Ugly Duckling thought he would die when one of the dogs found him. Then – splash – the dog turned and went.

"I'm so ugly!" thought the Ugly Duckling. "Even the dog does not bite me." And he went on his way, until he came to a hut where an old woman lived with her cat and a hen. Nobody saw him creeping inside . . .

The woman thought the Ugly Duckling was a lady duck to lay eggs for her. But as he grew fatter and uglier and no eggs came, she got angry. The hen and cat hated him because he could swim.

All summer long the Ugly Duckling was all alone, eating whatever he could find. Then came the autumn when the leaves blew down from the trees and the clouds hung low in the sky.

Then at sunset one day, the Ugly Duckling saw the most beautiful white birds flying across the lake. He watched them until they were out of sight, wishing with all his heart that he could be with them.

The winter snow reminded him of those beautiful white birds. The river froze, almost freezing the Ugly Duckling with it, until a kind man broke the ice and took him home.

His children wanted to play, but the Ugly Duckling thought they would hurt him. They scared him so much that he splashed into a pail of milk, and then into a barrel of oatmeal!

The children laughed and laughed, but their mother was furious. The Ugly Duckling only just missed being hit by the fire tongs, as he ran out into the bitter winter weather.

Now came the worst part of the Ugly Duckling's whole life. Often he felt he would die from hunger and cold, longing for some shelter. He could hardly believe it when the sun shone again, and birds sang.

Hearing the birds, the Ugly Duckling flapped his wings, surprised to find how big and strong they had become. The sun warmed his back as he flew,

making him feel happier than he had been for a long, long time.

On and on flew the Ugly Duckling until he saw a garden, the scent of flowers wafting up towards him. Suddenly, three beautiful white swans flew out from the thicket, gliding into the water.

These were the birds he had seen in the autumn, the ones he loved – although he did not know why. "What if they hurt me?" he thought. "Better to die here than to be beaten and punished because I'm so ugly . . ."

Slowly, the swans turned and came towards him, looking so solemn that the Ugly Duckling bowed his head. He saw his reflection in the water – not the reflection of an Ugly Duckling but of a beautiful white swan.

The Ugly Duckling thought he was dreaming! Could he really be a beautiful swan?

"There's a new swan! Isn't he lovely?" said some little children as they stood by the lake .

The handsome young swan lifted his head, looking all around him. "This cannot be a dream," he thought. "I could never have dreamed of being so happy when I was the Ugly Duckling!"

The Wizard of Oz

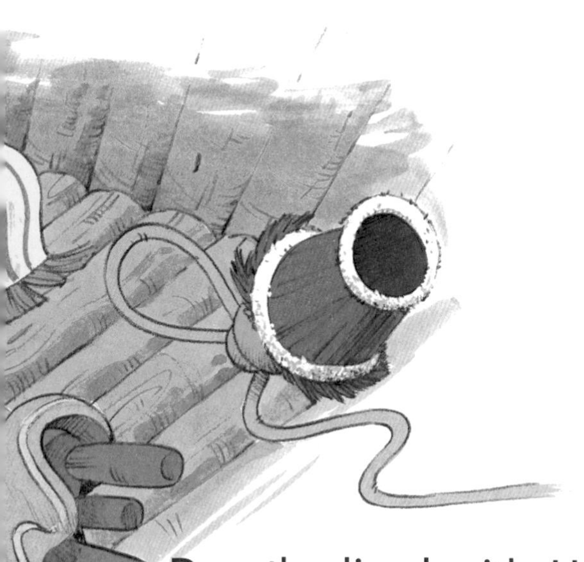

Dorothy lived with Uncle Henry and Aunt Em in Kansas, America. They were kind and hard-working, but they never smiled. It was Toto, Dorothy's little black dog, who made her laugh. One day, the sky grew dark, and from the north, the wind gave a howl. "A cyclone!" cried Aunt Em. "Run for the cellar!"

Dorothy did not know they were at the exact spot where the North and South winds met in the cyclone. She just managed to grab Toto before the whole house started shaking. Next minute, it rose up in the air!

As the house swayed and rocked, Dorothy fell asleep, waking up only when it stopped. She opened the door, looking out at a beautiful place with fruit trees, birds and a brook rippling between banks of flowers.

"Welcome to Munchkin Land!" came a voice, and three strange little folk came towards her with a pretty young woman. The three little men wore tall, pointed hats with bells around the brims.

"Your house fell on the Wicked Witch of the East and killed her!" cried the woman. "You've set the Munchkins free!" The men nodded, the bells on their hats tinkling madly. "They are slaves no longer!"

The woman said she was the Good Witch of the North. "Will you help me to get home?" asked Dorothy.

"The Wizard of Oz in Emerald City will help you," said the witch. "Follow the Yellow Brick Road!" The witch gave Dorothy a pair of magic shoes and a magic kiss to protect her. Then Dorothy put some fruit and a loaf in a basket and set off. It seemed a long, long way to go.

She saw the scarecrow when she sat on a fence to rest. "How do you do?" he said. Dorothy was amazed he could talk! She told him she was going to see the Wizard of Oz and he asked if he might come, too.

"He might give me a brain," he said, "instead of a head of straw!" Further along the road, they met a Tin Man with an axe. He wanted the wizard to give him a heart. "Nobody can love without one," he sighed.

So they all went on together. Suddenly, a huge lion came from nowhere. One blow of his paw toppled the scarecrow over, then he knocked the Tin Man to the ground. Then the lion went to bite Toto!

"A big lion like you, biting Toto," cried Dorothy. "What a coward!" The lion sighed. "I know. People usually run away when I roar." They couldn't help feeling sorry for him. Perhaps the Wizard would give him courage?

A green glow in the sky told them they were near the Emerald City. At the end of the Yellow Brick Road was a gate. Dorothy rang the bell and a little man appeared. "We've come to see the Wizard of Oz!" she said.

The man gave them spectacles as protection against the brightness of the green marble buildings, sparkling with emeralds. Most splendid of all was the palace, home of the Wizard of Oz.

The throne room was magnificent, with a bright light shining down on all the emeralds. In the centre was a throne with a giant head set in its huge back. "I am the Wizard of Oz!" it boomed. "Why do you seek me?"

Dorothy explained what had happened and how she wanted to get home. But the Wizard said she must first kill the Wicked Witch of the West! If the Tin Man, scarecrow and the lion helped her, they would get what they wanted, too.

"Keep to the West!" said the man at the gate. "You'll find her where the sun sets!" But the witch already knew Dorothy and her friends were on their way. She blew a whistle to call a pack of wolves.

"Get to those people!" she screamed. "Tear them to pieces!" The lion, the Tin Man and the scarecrow heard the wolves coming. "Get behind me!" cried the Tin Man. "It's my fight!" And with his axe, he killed them all.

Then a large flock of wild crows appeared. "Tear the strangers to pieces!" screamed the witch. But the scarecrow spread out his arms to catch them all! Next the witch put on a golden hat.

Three winged monkeys appeared. "Kill the strangers!" she cried. "Except the lion. He'll be my slave!" The Tin Man was thrown over rocks, straw was pulled out of the scarecrow... but the brave lion would not work as a slave.

Dorothy could not be harmed because she was protected by magic. So the witch put her to work, and kicking Toto out of the way, tried to get the magic shoes. Dorothy was so angry, she flung a pail of water over her!

The witch melted into a puddle for Dorothy to mop up! Then she put on the magic cap and asked the monkeys to help mend the scarecrow and the Tin Man and take them back to Oz. There was an old man in the throne room.

He said that he had gone up in a balloon one day and when he landed in Oz, everyone thought he was a wizard! He gave the Tin Man a satin heart, and the scarecrow a certificate to show how clever he was.

The lion was given a drink. "Once it's inside you," said the man, "it will be courage. That always comes from the inside." He smiled to himself. Each of them had already shown he was clever, kind and brave.

Dorothy still wanted her wish. So the monkeys took them all to Glinda, the Good Witch of the South, who told Dorothy to click her heels three times. She said goodbye and shouted, "Take me home!"

She felt herself whirling through the air then rolling over on the grass. "My darling child!" cried Aunt Em. "Where did you come from?" "The Land of Oz!" said Dorothy. "Oh, Aunt Em. I AM glad to be home!"

Pinocchio

Geppetto was a poor toymaker whose dearest wish had always been to have a son. One day, as he sat at his work-bench making a wooden puppet, it seemed to look at him and to smile. "How I wish I could look on the face of my son," he said. "I would call him Pinocchio."

Geppetto did not know it, but the Blue Fairy had heard what he said.

"He deserves to have his wish granted," she thought. "Pinocchio shall be a son to Geppetto."

And, as Pinocchio's eyes opened wide, so there came a chirruping noise from the fireplace. "Meet Jiminy Cricket!" said the fairy. "He is your conscience to tell you right from wrong, Pinocchio."

Geppetto was overjoyed to have a son at last! "You must go to school, Pinocchio," he said.

"That's right!" nodded Jiminy Cricket. "Otherwise, you'll turn into a donkey."

Geppetto even sold his only jacket so that he could buy Pinocchio the spelling book he needed to take to school.

"Goodbye, Father!" he called. "I shall make you proud of me."

But that was before Pinocchio knew Fire-Eater's Puppet Theatre was in town! Taking no notice of Jiminy Cricket, he sold his book to buy a ticket – and soon he was on stage, singing and dancing.

Fire-Eater wanted Pinocchio to stay. But when the time came to move far away from home and Geppetto, he was afraid. Being a wonderful singing, dancing puppet didn't seem so clever, after all. . .

"Geppetto sold his jacket to send me to school," he sobbed to Jiminy Cricket. "He'll wonder where I am!"

Luckily for him, Fire-Eater knew Geppetto and he gave Pinocchio five pieces of gold to take home to him!

"I can buy Geppetto a new jacket," cried Pinocchio. "Five gold pieces!"

"Is that all?" scoffed a cat.

"Bury them in our magic field," said the fox with him. "You'll have a tree of gold next day!"

"No, Pinocchio!" said Jiminy Cricket. "That's Geppetto's money!"

How Pinocchio wished he had listened to Jiminy when he discovered that the crafty cat and the sly fox had dug up the gold he had buried!

The fairy heard Pinocchio crying and asked him what was wrong.

"I dropped the gold I was taking home to Geppetto," he sobbed. "Now I can't find it!" And as he spoke, something very strange happened. . .

Pinocchio's nose began to grow!

"Where do you think you lost the money?" asked the fairy.

"On the way to school," he cried. His nose grew even longer! "It must have fallen out of my pocket."

By now, his nose was so long, he could hardly see the end of it!

"Well, Pinocchio," laughed the Blue Fairy, "now you know how one small lie can grow into a big lie – just like your nose!"

At once, Pinocchio promised not to tell any more lies, sobbing so hard that the fairy took pity on him. "If you had listened to Jiminy Cricket," she said, "none of this would have happened!"

Pinocchio knew this was true, and, full of good intentions, he set off home. He had only gone a little way when a carriage full of children came along, pulled by some strange-looking donkeys!

"Come to the Land of Toys!" they cried. "Play all the year round!"

"Don't listen to them," warned Jiminy Cricket. But Pinocchio was already jumping up, determined not to miss any of the fun.

He thought the Land of Toys was wonderful! No books, no lessons – just as much play as anyone wanted!

But after a while, he noticed his ears felt rather heavy – heavy and long, thick and furry . . .

"I said that you'd turn into a donkey if you didn't go to school," scolded Jiminy Cricket. "What will you do, now?"

"Geppetto!" cried Pinocchio. "I want to go home to Geppetto!"

Pinocchio was afraid everyone would laugh at his donkey ears. But the people were too upset even to notice. "Geppetto went to sea, looking for you," they said. "We think he was swallowed by a whale!"

"Poor Father," cried Pinocchio. "I must find him!" He made his way to the place where Geppetto was last seen and jumped into the inky blackness of the sea, gusts of wind hitting him in the face.

Suddenly, he saw a light ahead. He swam towards it and found himself crawling, then walking into a sort of underground cavern. "Pinocchio!" cried a voice. "Pinocchio, my dear, brave son!"

Pinocchio had never been so glad to see anyone – even if he had swum inside a whale by mistake!

"We'll get through the whale's mouth, then make for the shore," he told Geppetto. "Just follow me!"

When the whale opened its mouth, they were out! But Pinocchio was soon very tired, swimming for Geppetto as well as himself. By the time Jiminy Cricket had guided him to dry land, he could hardly move.

The Blue Fairy was waiting when Geppetto carried him to dry land.

"Well done, Pinocchio," she said. "You have shown that you are a brave and loving son. You shall have your reward!"

And instead of a wooden puppet, Pinocchio became a real boy with a beaming smile for Geppetto – and a conscience of his own to tell him right from wrong. How happy Jiminy Cricket was for both his friends!

Stories I have read

- *Goldilocks and the Three Bears* ☐
- *Red Riding Hood* ☐
- *Snow White and the Seven Dwarfs* ☐
- *The Ugly Duckling* ☐
- *The Wizard of Oz* ☐
- *Pinocchio* ☐